THIS IS A BORZOI BOOK PUBLISHED BY ALFRED A. KNOPF, INC.
Copyright © 1992 by Leo Lionni
ISBN: 0-679-82464-2 (trade)   ISBN: 0-679-92464-7 (lib. bdg.)
Library of Congress Catalog Card Number: 91-29149
Manufactured in the United States of America
10 9 8 7 6 5 4 3 2 1

Leo Lionni

A Busy Year

Alfred A. Knopf · New York

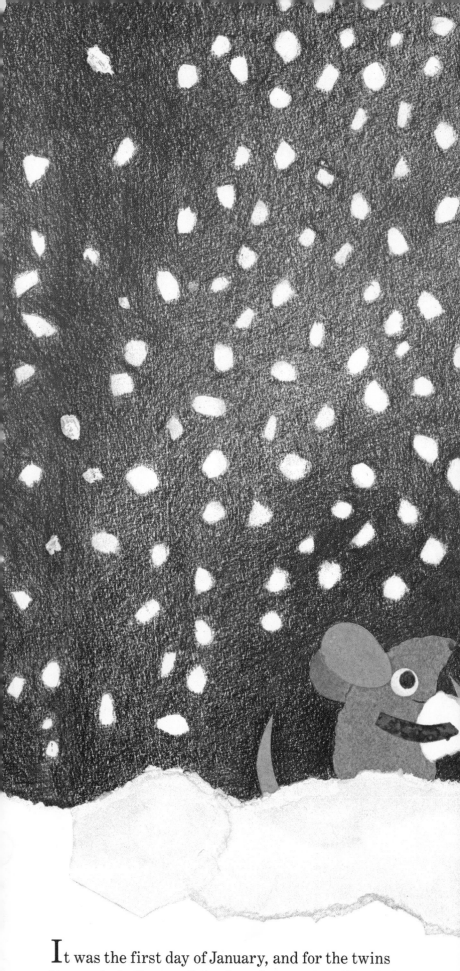

It was the first day of January, and for the twins it was their first walk in the winter snow. "Look," said Willie, "a snowmouse!" "He's holding a broom," said Winnie.

But then they heard a voice: "I am not a broom.
I am Woody the tree!" The twins couldn't believe
their ears. A talking tree!

When they returned a few weeks later, it was already February, and the snowmouse was melting away. But the tree was still there. "What have you two been up to?" she asked.

The twins told Woody about the McBarney barn where they lived, and about the cows and the horses and the chickens who lived there too.

In March the rain and the wind never seemed to stop, but the twins went to see Woody just the same. She had become their friend.

"All this rain is fine," she said. "I need it.
And soon it will be Spring. I can't wait. I feel
my buds."

And, indeed, when April came, Woody's branches were full of buds. "How do you know which ones

will be the blossoms and which ones the leaves?"
Winnie wondered. To her they all looked the same.

"Oh, Woody, you're beautiful!" said the twins when they returned in May. "Yes," said Woody, her branches heavy with blossoms and leaves.

"May is my month!" It was warm, and the three
friends talked and played all day. On their way home
Willie said, "It's a shame that Woody can't run."

"You look sad," said the twins when they saw Woody again. "Don't you like June and the summertime?" "I do," said Woody, "but people are careless with cigarettes and campfires,

and many trees die in the flames. And I can't run."
The twins looked at each other. "Don't worry,
Woody, we'll protect you," they said as they ran
back to the barn to find a hose and water.

It was July when one morning Winnie and Willie
heard screams. "Help! Help! Fire!" It was Woody.
They unrolled the hose as fast as they could.

The flames had almost reached their friend, but the twins arrived just in time. "Winnie, Willie, how can I ever thank you!" said Woody gratefully.

August was vacation month. The twins went to the
seashore with their parents, but first they went to
say good-bye to Woody. Woody was sound asleep.

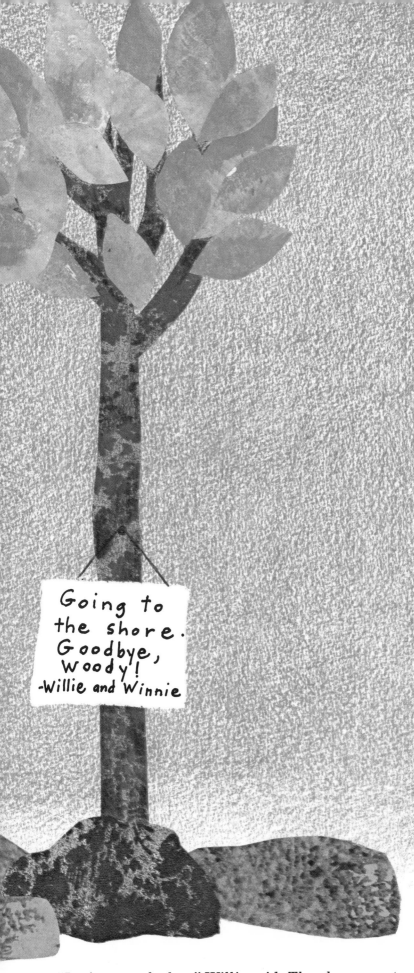

"Let's not wake her," Willie said. They hung a note from her bark. It said: "Going to the shore. Good-bye, Woody!"

When they returned in September, Woody's branches were full of fragrant, juicy fruit. "How busy you've been!" the twins exclaimed.

"Take as many as you want," said Woody, and the
twins ate their bellies full. Nothing had ever
tasted so good.

October arrived. Autumn was almost gone, and
Winter was coming closer. Icy winds blew Woody's
leaves away. "Poor Woody," said the twins.

"Don't worry," said Woody. "Next year I'll have new leaves. You'll see!"

The tree was bare now. "It's November already,"
Willie whispered. "What shall we give Woody for
Christmas?" "She deserves the best," said Winnie.
"I shall give her a nice piece of cheese."

Willie looked at her with dismay. "Cheese?"
he said. "Trees don't eat cheese." "I know,"
said Winnie, laughing. "But it's the thought
that counts."

December came . . . and then it was Christmas.
Winnie stepped forward to give Woody her
present. "What is it?" asked Willie. "Manure!"
said Winnie triumphantly. "Disgusting," said
Willie. But Woody laughed. "Fertilizer is
just what I need." And she meant it.

Then it was Willie's turn. His box was full
of bulbs and flower seeds to plant around
the tree. Woody thanked her two friends.
"Merry Christmas!" they all shouted together.
They were happy and ready for another
busy year.